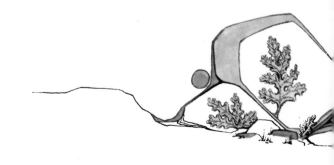

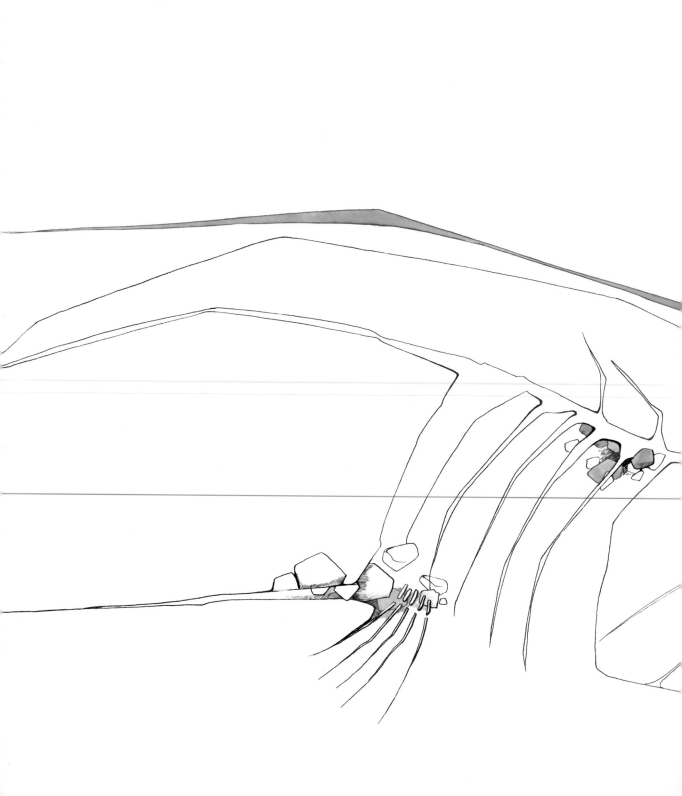

IF YOU ARE
A HUNTER OF FOSSILS

BYRD BAYLOR / PETER PARNALL

Aladdin Paperbacks

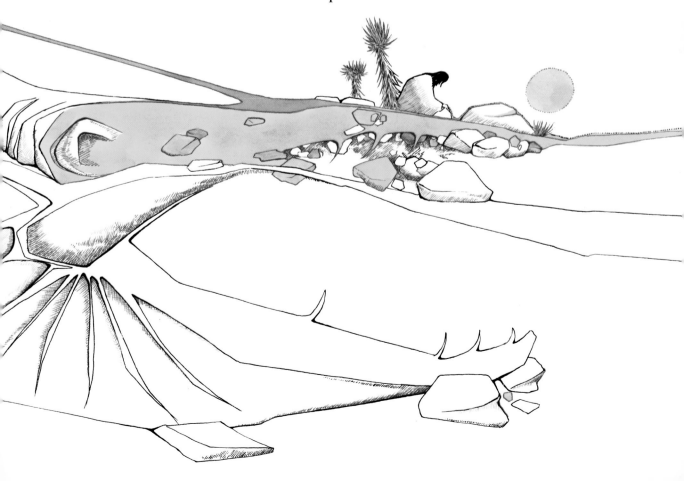

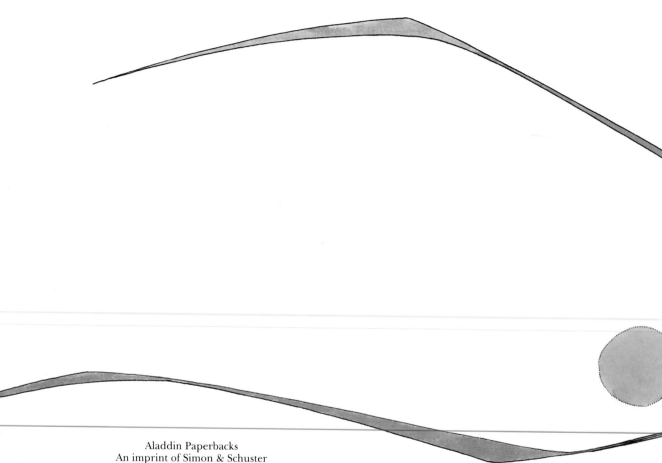

Aladdin Paperbacks
An imprint of Simon & Schuster
Children's Publishing Division
1230 Avenue of the Americas
New York, NY 10020

Library of Congress Cataloging in Publication Data
Baylor, Byrd.
If you are a hunter of fossils.
SUMMARY: A fossil hunter looking for signs of an
ancient sea in the rocks of a western Texas mountain
describes how the area must have looked millions
of years ago.
[1. Geology—Fiction]   I. Parnall, Peter.
II. Title.
PZ7.B3435If   [E]   79-17926
ISBN 0-689-70773-8

Printed in Hong Kong

15   14   13   12   11   10

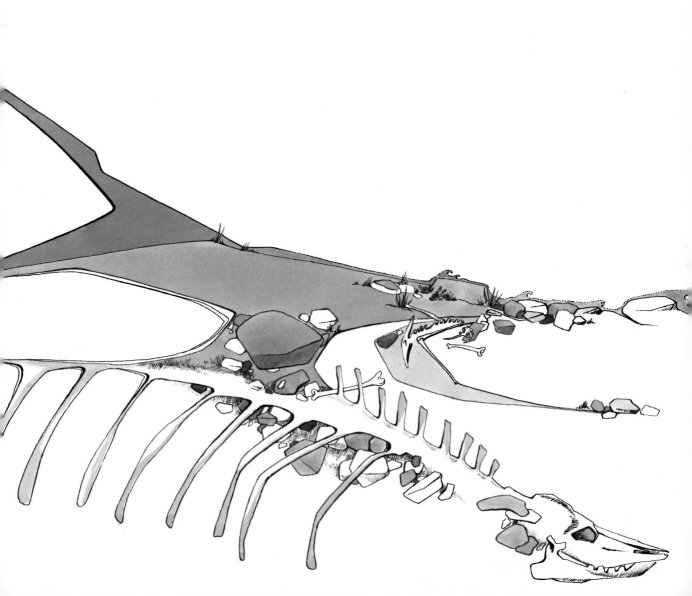

To Jim Baylor

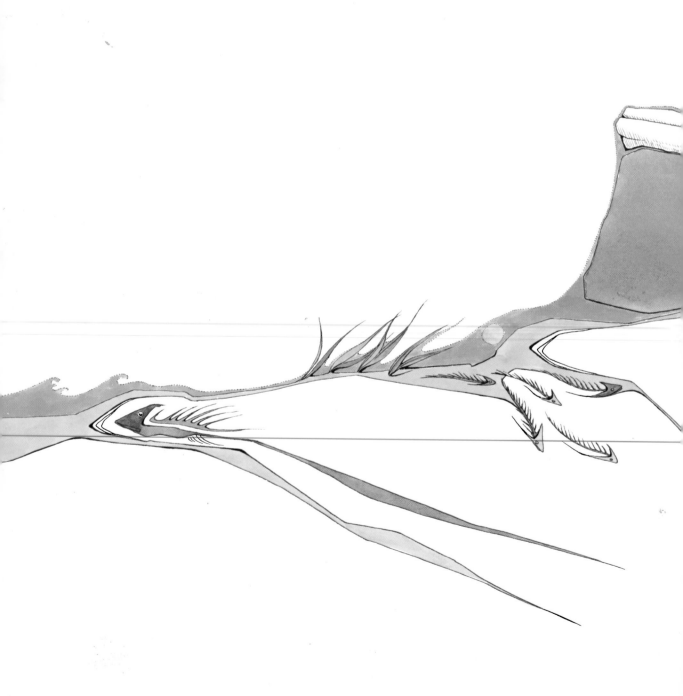

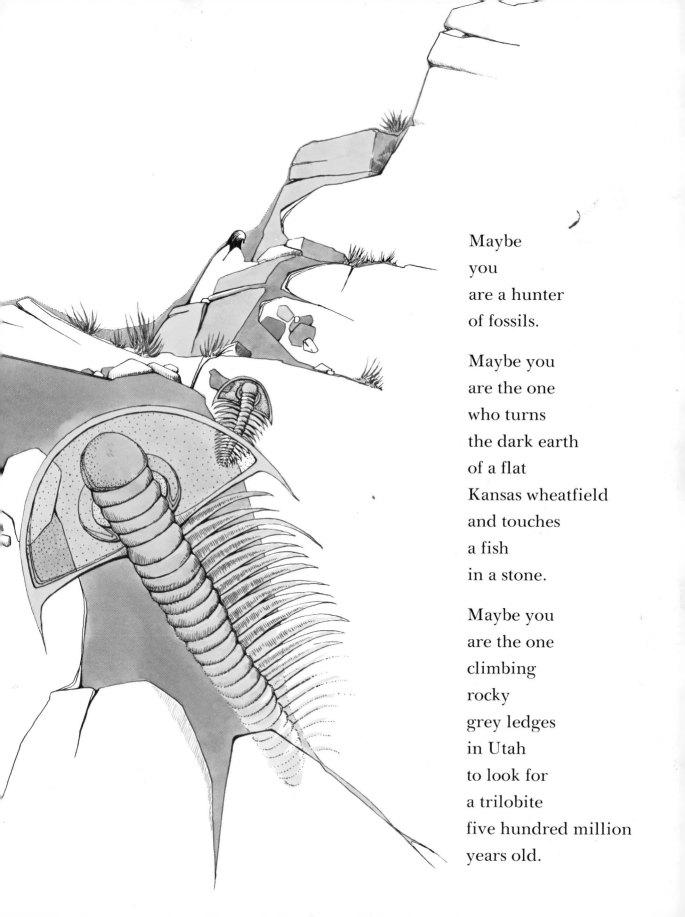

Maybe
you
are a hunter
of fossils.

Maybe you
are the one
who turns
the dark earth
of a flat
Kansas wheatfield
and touches
a fish
in a stone.

Maybe you
are the one
climbing
rocky
grey ledges
in Utah
to look for
a trilobite
five hundred million
years old.

Maybe you
are the one
in Wyoming
with your feet
in a dinosaur track

or the one
who finds
a seed fern
in Pennsylvania shale,
so perfect
every
vein
still shows.

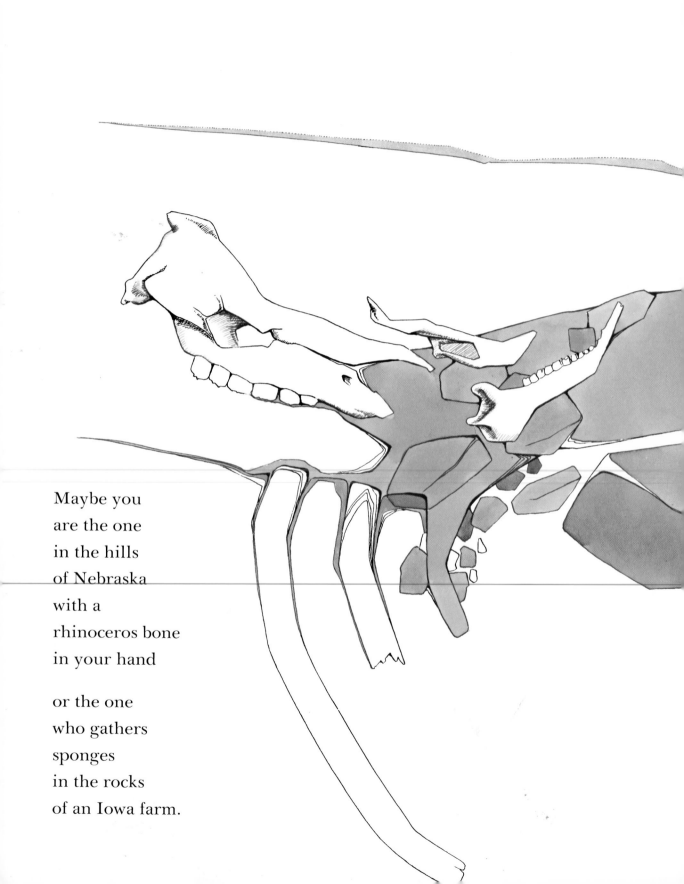

Maybe you
are the one
in the hills
of Nebraska
with a
rhinoceros bone
in your hand

or the one
who gathers
sponges
in the rocks
of an Iowa farm.

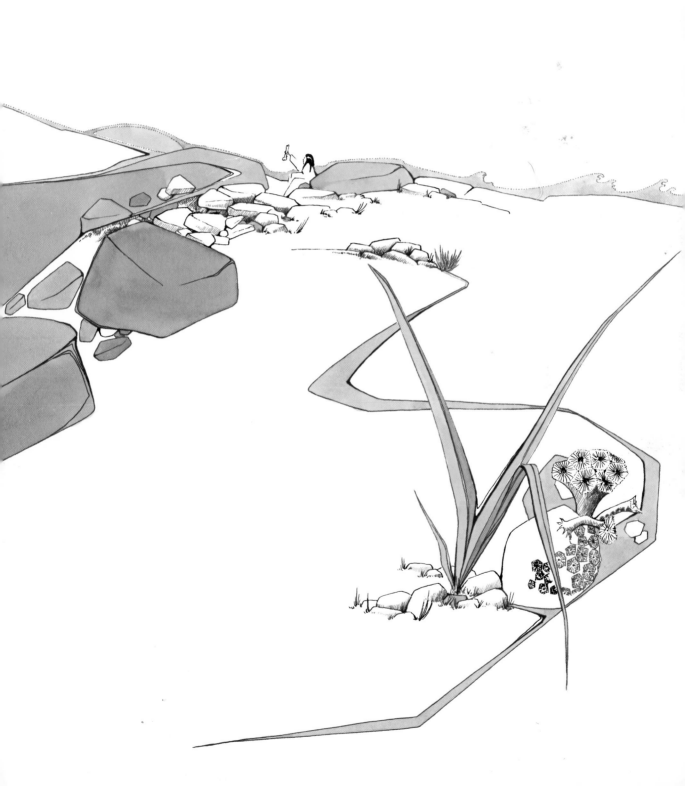

Maybe you
are a hunter of fossils—
like me.

I am the one
on the side of
a West Texas
mountain

reading
the rocks

looking
for signs
of the sea
that was
here.

Today
you'd find me
resting
on a chalky
limestone boulder
by a prickly pear.

There are
seashells
in this rock,
jumbled,
jammed together,
large and small.

I always stop
and touch
the ones that
curl
like
little ram's horns.
(*Exogyra*
is their name.)

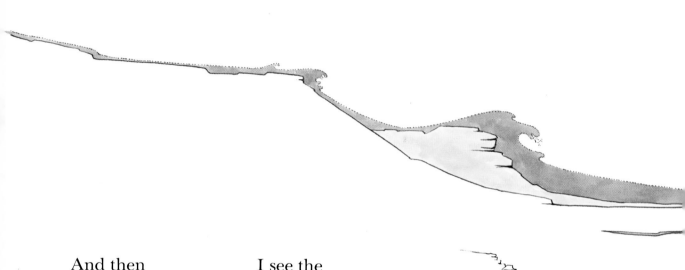

And then
I sit here
in the sun
resting
from
the long
steep
climb.

I see the
ranchland
down below—
the clumps
of cactus
and the tall
pale yuccas
and the dry grass
bending
in the wind.

I see the
salt flats
and the
dust devils
blowing

and the dirt road
going
to a windmill
and one
blue
pickup truck
moving
slowly
down that road.

But that
seems
far away   and not quite real.

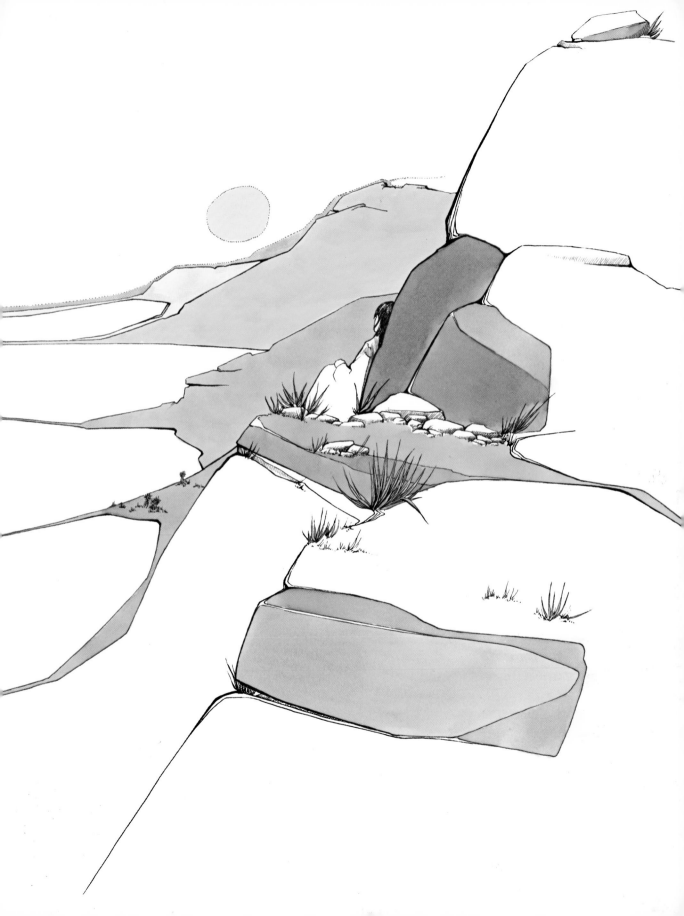

Up here,
what's *real*
is the
shallow
warm
Cretaceous sea
that all these
seashells
knew.

On this mountain,
every rock
still holds
the memory of
that time.
When you are here,
you hold it too.

The ocean's
salt
is in your blood.
Its lime
is in your bones.
Its waves
rise
slow and green
around you
and you feel
the pull
of tides.

It never seems
to be
now.

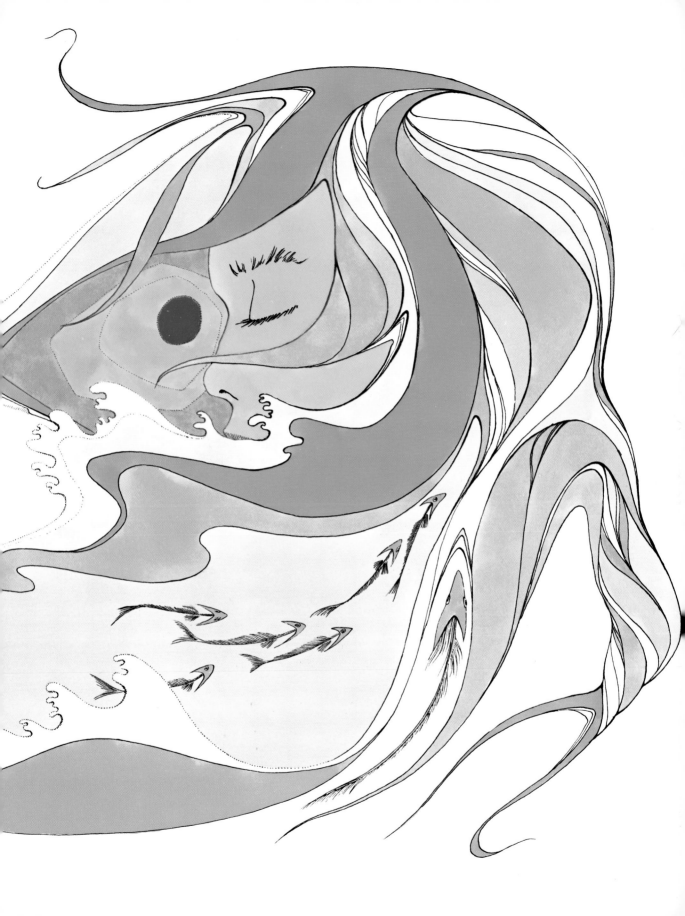

Here,
time flows back
and forth
so easily
that
any day
can be
wrapped up
inside
some other day
that came
and went
a hundred million
years ago.

Here,
when I find
a brachiopod
or mollusk
or a round
sea urchin,
I don't just
see it
as it is…
on a mountain
locked
in rock.

I see it
in that
ancient
lapping
water.

I see
the tiny
clams
plowing
through mud.
I see
sea lillies
sway.

I see
all the creatures
with shells
and plates
and spines.
Slow moving,
glimmering,
they hide
in the crevices,

creep
into holes
in the rocks.

I see the
waving tentacles
and curving
spiral shells
of ammonites.
It is their day.
They are
the masters of
this sunken
sea-floor world.

Above them,
fish
swim lazily
by coral reefs.
Sharks
move
through
darkness.

It is an age
of reptiles
in the sea,
of giant turtles
and great serpents,
sharp-toothed
monsters,
swimming lizards
forty feet long.

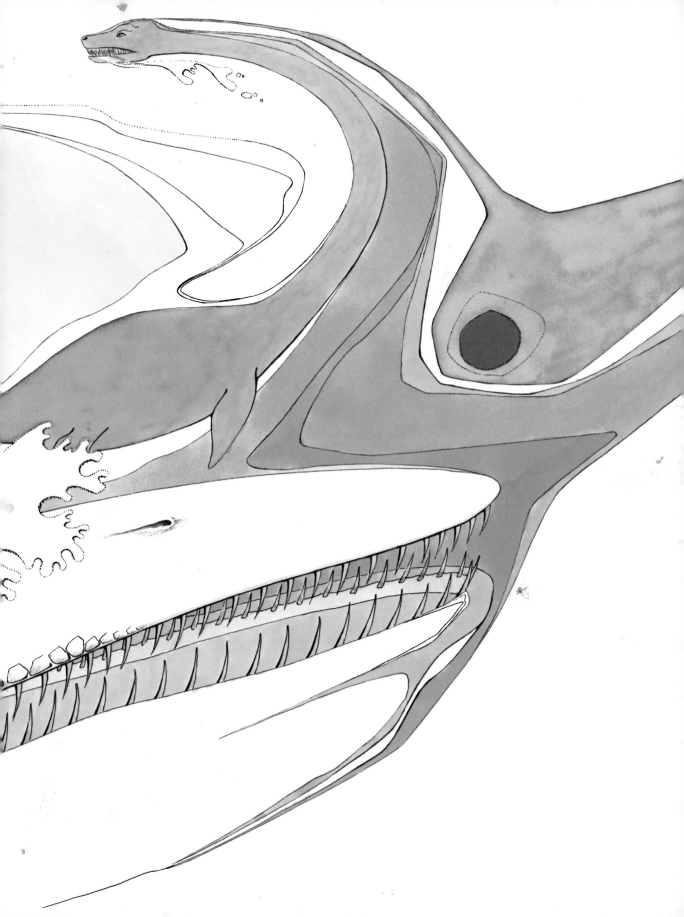

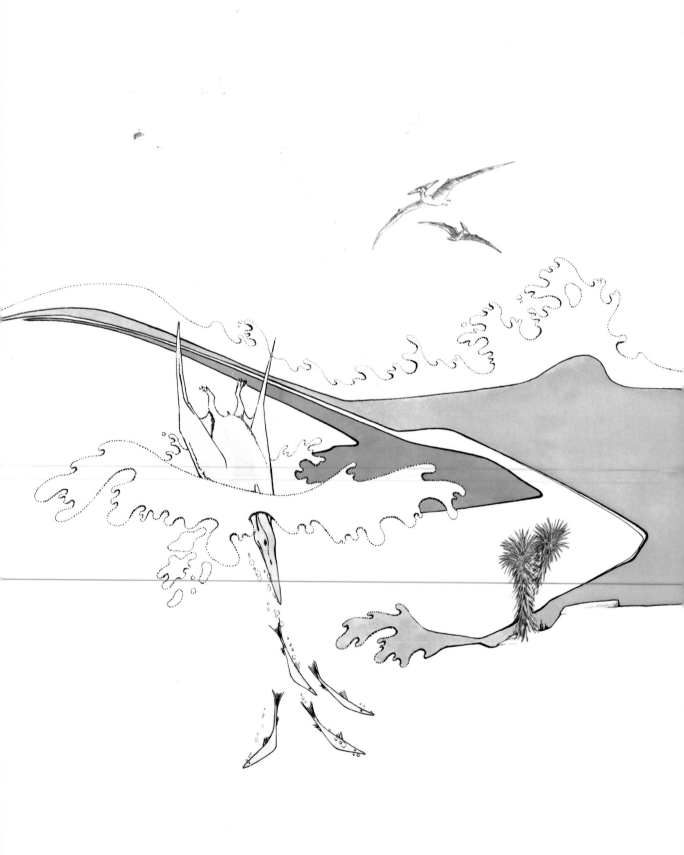

And in the air
above the waves,
a reptile
named
Pteranodon
flaps its long
grey
bat-like wings
and dives
for food.
No animal
so large
has ever flown—
before that time
or since.

But on this
mountain,
any little wind
brings back
the sound
of those fog-grey wings
still flapping.

Up here,
you never are
surprised
by things like
that.

Sometimes
you even feel
the long
slow
terror
in that world
when water
turned
to mud.

It took
millions of years
for ocean slime
and sun
to fight it out

but
finally
sunshine
won.

Now
that sea is
a mountain of
rock
that I climb
with a shell
in my hand.

If you are
a hunter of fossils
you know
how the day
always
ends.

You know
how it is
to go home
feeling glad
that you walk
in the sun…
breathing
air.

You always
walk home
kind of proud.

You always
hold on
to that long
chain of life
as you
go.

Byrd Baylor and Peter Parnall have collaborated on three Caldecott Honor books: *The Desert Is Theirs; Hawk, I'm Your Brother;* and *The Way To Start a Day.*

Byrd Baylor lives in the Southwest. Her eloquent lyric prose reflects a philosophy as special and lovely as the lands she writes about. For her it is the spirit — not material things — that is necessary for personal development. "Once you make that decision, your whole life opens up and you begin to know what matters and what doesn't."

Peter Parnall lives on a farm in Maine with his wife and two children. His drawings have been described as stunning, glittering and breathtaking. When he draws the animal world, he has an uncanny ability to portray that world as the animals themselves might experience it.